Dear Parent:
Your child's love of reading starts here!

Every child learns to read in a different way and at his or her own speed. Some go back and forth between reading levels and read favorite books again and again. Others read through each level in order. You can help your young reader improve and become more confident by encouraging his or her own interests and abilities. From books your child reads with you to the first books he or she reads alone, there are I Can Read Books for every stage of reading:

SHARED READING
Basic language, word repetition, and whimsical illustrations, ideal for sharing with your emergent reader

BEGINNING READING
Short sentences, familiar words, and simple concepts for children eager to read on their own

READING WITH HELP
Engaging stories, longer sentences, and language play for developing readers

READING ALONE
Complex plots, challenging vocabulary, and high-interest topics for the independent reader

ADVANCED READING
Short paragraphs, chapters, and exciting themes for the perfect bridge to chapter books

I Can Read Books have introduced children to the joy of reading since 1957. Featuring award-winning authors and illustrators and a fabulous cast of beloved characters, I Can Read Books set the standard for beginning readers.

A lifetime of discovery begins with the magical words **"I Can Read!"**

Visit www.icanread.com for information
on enriching your child's reading experience.

OPEN SEASON™

Meet the Characters

HarperCollins®, ☰®, and I Can Read Book® are trademarks of HarperCollins Publishers.

Open Season: Meet the Characters

™ & © 2006 Sony Pictures Animation, Inc. All rights reserved.

Printed in the United States of America.

No part of this book may be used or reproduced in any manner whatsoever without written permission except in the case of brief quotations embodied in critical articles and reviews. Printed in the United States of America. For information address HarperCollins Children's Books, a division of HarperCollins Publishers, 1350 Avenue of the Americas, New York, NY 10019. www.icanread.com

Library of Congress catalog card number: 2006926604

ISBN-10: 0-06-084606-2 — ISBN-13: 978-0-06-084606-0

❖   First Edition

OPEN SEASON™

Meet the Characters

Adapted by Monique Z. Stephens

HarperCollins *Publishers*

It is open season

in the town of Timberline.

For the creatures living in the forest,

open season has always meant

two things:

the hunters against the animals,

and every animal for himself!

But this season,

the animals join together.

They fight back and they win!

And it all started with a bear named Boog

and a deer named Elliot.

This is Boog.

He looks like a bear.

He moves like a bear.

He is a bear.

But Boog is different.

Boog has been raised
by Park Ranger Beth
since he was a wee little cub.
Beth is Boog's human mom!

Boog can ride in a truck.

He performs in a show.

He even knows how to use a toilet!

But Boog does not know

how to roar loudly like a bear should.

He does not know how to catch fish

or live on his own in the wild.

But why should Boog care about that?

He loves Beth and Beth loves him.

His life is perfect . . .

. . . until the day Boog meets Elliot.

Elliot is a deer.

He looks like a deer.

He moves like a deer.

He knows how to do everything
that a deer should do.

Elliot has only one problem.

Well, he has two problems.

Oops, wrong again.

He has three problems!

First, he was kicked out of the herd by a bully named Ian.

Next, Elliot was caught

by a mean hunter named Shaw.

To top it all off,

one of his antlers broke off!

Elliot needs a friend.

Boog can be his friend!

But first he needs Boog to set him free

from the hood of Shaw's truck

before that crazy hunter returns.

This is Shaw.

He hates all the animals.

He thinks they are working together
and plotting against him.

Boog slashes through the ropes
with his claws.

Rippp!

Elliot is free!

Will Boog be his buddy now?

Will Boog come with Elliot

to the forest

to live like a real bear?

"No way!" says Boog.

He does not want to be Elliot's friend.

He does not want to live in the wild.

Boog likes things just the way they are.

Then something terrible happens.

Beth takes Boog

to go live in the forest!

Beth knows it is time for Boog

to learn how to live on his own.

At first Boog is sadder
than he has ever been.
All he can think about
is returning to Beth.

But soon he meets the other animals.

There's McSquizzy and his squirrel clan,

Reilly and his beaver construction crew,

the rabbits, the skunks, and Giselle,

the most beautiful doe in the forest.

The animals tease Boog because
he does not know how to be a real bear.

Even the beavers make fun of him.

Then open season begins.

The hunters come.

There is no safe place to hide.

Boog knows there is only

one thing to do—

get all the animals

to fight back!

With Boog as their leader,

the animals work together.

Boog grabs a plunger.

Elliot grabs a can of spray cheese.

The rabbits

get forks and knives.

Every animal

pitches in.

And the hunters

run away!

Boog still misses Beth.

She will always be his mom.

But now he has a new family,

new friends, and a new home

in the forest, where he belongs!